THE LAST CLOUD

THE LAST CLOUD

Yet Another
Pretentious Collection of Very Short Works

by

K.M. Halpern

Ɛpsilon Books

ISBN-13 (paperback): 978-1-945671-15-9

ISBN-13 (ebook): 978-1-945671-16-6

Library of Congress Control Number: 2020936125

Published by Epsilon Books

Printed in the United States of America

Cover Art by Richie Montgomery

First Edition (rev 1)

CONTENTS

The Last Cloud

The sky had been ominous, portentous gray scattering wet. But then it cleared, as skies do. In the distance I espied something adrift, receding ever so slowly. It was a little cloud, a lone straggler gently wafting its way without a care in the world.

A sorrow overtook me. What if this was it, something which never again could be? What if this was the last cloud? Perhaps the last in the world or the last in my city or the last in my life?

That which came before need not come again, and the most reliable of clocks has a final stroke. So many clouds have crossed my mind's sky, it is tempting to believe there always will be another. Another moment, another memory, another cloud. But only a fool assumes such things.

Some cloud will be the last. This could be it. From now until time's end, my firmament would be empty. No billowing form would invite me to daydream, no gentle tuft would keep me company, if but for the span of a sigh. Nothing would dim, however briefly, the sun's execrable malice. Nothing would stand between me and the deadly cold infinity of beyond.

I knew this was it. Somehow I knew. A thousand years from now, they would remember me but not it. I would be the man who saw the last cloud. I too would be the last of a kind. Or perhaps another would claim credit. Who could contest such a thing?

Suddenly I sensed a shadow, small and hesitant. It was a tiny cloud, nascent, filled with possibility. I breathed deep of relief. I was not ready for the end, however much I imagined myself so.

A Wonderful Day in the Neighborhood

Shot

Huh?

Shot

What the fuck?

Shot

Oh yeah, baby

Shot

Fucking hell

Shot

That's awesome

Shot

Scum had it comin'

Shot

Not by me

Shot

My boy!???!!

Shot

Hell's bells that's nasty

Shot

Guts

Shot

Where da cops at?

Shot

Guts everywhere

Shot

Stop your bawling

Shot

That's fucked up, man

Shot

Like that shit don't happen to all of us

Shot

That's gotta hurt

Shot

...awful lot of blood...

Shot

Who gives a fuck

Shot

A-hole don't got no aim

Shot

Piece of shit bleeding all over, giving us a bad rep

Shot

His own fault for being on that corner

Shot

Who did it?

Shot

Who didn't?

Knowing

The wise man says I don't know.
The logician says I can't know.
The realist says I won't know.
The success says I don't want to know.
The laborer says I don't need to know.
The ideologue says I know.
The lunatic knows.

A Sordid Affair

It was a sordid affair by all accounts, but those accounts most likely were overdrawn so let's pay them little mind. As it happened, the details emerged, as details do, in their own time. This is to say that all speculation was premature, but preemptively ascertained the fault in the sordid affair and attributed blame accordingly. Only when all parties were long past censure or recompense did censure or recompense prove necessary, as it inevitably does when there is a preemptive attribution of fault. It was indeed a sordid affair.

Undulating

There's something undulating. I don't like it when something undulates. Not a specific something, but a general something, an anything. When anything undulates I feel uncomfortable. What is causing it to undulate. Is it worms or maggots or catchy music. Is it the convulsing flesh of disease or madness or is it just absentminded? As the philosopher once said right before impaling himself, the purpose of life is to hear the undulations of the women. This is why they undulate silently. To lend purpose to life would be a desecration. Everyone and everything undulates and this disturbs me, for I don't like it when something or anything or nothing undulates. Sometimes I think that something or anything or nothing undulates solely to disturb me. Even the word undulate undulates in its own quiet, obscene way.

Condonation

I don't condone violence and I am deeply deeply sorry for your loss and my thoughts and prayers are with you and your family and we have no comment at this time and our service has fallen short of our usual high standards of customer care and your call is very important to us and we do hope you had a wonderful trip and your opinion is valuable to us and we know you'll want to share this with friends and family and I've decided to spend more time with my family and we welcome you to our experience and please take a moment to fill out this survey and customer safety is our number one concern and we have an important message from our sponsors and you're a winner and after a careful internal investigation we found that all policies were followed. I don't condone violence because there is no one to be violent toward, just endlessly recycled words mumbled into darkness.

The Way Home

There are sixteen bridges between a man and enlighten-ment.

This isn't going to be cheap.   The fluxxle rod is broken.

They must be crossed in the correct order or no order at all.

And there's wear and tear on your pinter shaft. That needs to be taken care of.

One false crossing and the pattern must be restarted.

I'll give it to you straight. It's just not safe. I mean, I'm surprised you're still alive.

But it cannot be restarted, for all things have a single start if many ends.

Sure some people would be willing to do *some* of the repairs, would let you skimp. The sort of people willing to take your money, knowing you'd walk out with a death-trap.

Thus you must find a way to undo that which has been done, and there only is one way.

I'm not like that. I do it right. So no, it's all or nothing. But if you want to cheap out, by all means go down the street to Al's or Bob's or Falligan the Flayer's.

To each lock a single key, even if that lock was closed in ignorance.

Because we stake a lot on our reputation. I see you know what I mean.

But you have more locks than you imagine, and more keys still. Yet do not try them with abandon.

So what will it be pal? You've lucked out and I've got a slot this afternoon, but nothing after that for three months.

For a key in the wrong lock is a wrong crossing. It cannot be undone, only compensated for.

Of course, you'll have to leave it here. I'll let you know if I see anything else that needs work.

The unwary traveler soon will find they owe a debt to the world which cannot be repaid.

You wouldn't want me to skimp on your safety, would you?

All that then remains is to wander and cross and recross in the vain hope that you one day will balance the books.

But you came to the right place. Don't worry, we'll sort out payment later.

The books never are balanced. It is not that this cannot happen. It does not happen.

Doreen will send an invoice.

Once ensnared, every motion — however slight — tightens the coils.

Trust me pal, you're doing the right thing. I'd hate to be caught in that thing the way it is.

It is best not to move at all, unless you know the correct order.

I've seen what can happen. Believe me, you don't want that happening to you.

And you both will and can cross the bridges in the correct order or no order at all.

But you're in good hands. I'll sort out your fluxxle rod and pinter shaft and anything else that's wrong.

But if you could do that, you already would have.

And you can pay afterward.

And there would be no sixteen bridges between you and enlightenment.

In installments.

Chagrin

Chagrin begins with a grin
at the wrong person at the
wrong time for the wrong
reason in the wrong place.
A little better, faster,
smoother, prettier, and
there would be no chagrin.
Yet.

Superior

The key to sanctimony is to truly believe yourself
superior. But what happens when two sanctimo-
nious men meet? There is nothing perplexing in this.
Both think themselves superior. This is the marvel
of thinking oneself superior. There can be only one
who is superior, but no limit to those who imagine
themselves so.

Well Being

I stand on the edge of the well, peering into that circle of perfect imperfect darkness, a shimmering glimmer of maybe disturbance, the hint of reflection waiting to reach up and pull me in, draw me to her, crumble the stone hedge not meant to hedge, on which my life balances precariously, though perhaps not, because who knows how deep the hole goes and what really lies at the bottom, perhaps a mere scrape or sprain or knee-deep in some muck to awkwardly confess at a party, or maybe clawing for days on slime begging calling screaming for someone anyone but not her, I don't want to be with her after all, a part of her, drawn into her, but nobody answers as all I am wastes and shrivels to an emaciation pretending it isn't dead but knowing otherwise, never-ending unknowing otherwise. Or maybe I'll find a penny.

Violation

Violation! You have committed a violation and there can be no mercy. You are a violator, someone who has violated. Such was your violation that nobody will forget, nobody will forgive. It will hound you to the imaginary end of imagining. There is nothing you can do. You have been caught, convicted, and soon will be punished.

Every violation must be punished. It does not matter why it is a violation or who declared it to be one. A violation cannot go uncaught, unconvicted, unpunished. Maybe yours was an accidental violation, an unwitting oversight. Yes, I'm sure it was. Liar, there is no such thing! A violation is a violation. Nothing may excuse it, nothing erase it.

From this moment until the end of your existence you will regret it. That existence will be miserable, that end will come soon.   You should not have committed the violation. Everyone knows this. Why did you do it? Who can fathom your arrogance, your stupidity. Surely there is some defect, some explanation. It is not the violation itself but what it portends, what it recommends.

You! You are a violator. The type of person who commits a violation. There are two types of people: those who violate and those who do not. No longer can you pass as innocent. All will know of your depravity. The opprobrium! The opprobrium!

If only you had stayed home, not been tempted, not displayed the true you, not shown the world what you are. A violator, a violation. They are the same, these. There can be no difference. No cause and effect, doer and doee.

As you live, or pretend to live, or fail to live, know this: every single person you pass sees what you are, what you did. All of them know what to think of you and will think it of you and can think nothing else of you. Did you do great deeds? Erased. Did you serve the community? Erased. Did you lovingly raise a family? Erased. All of these were lies, have been shown to be lies, are now known to be lies.

You are a violator. The type of person who commits a violation. You are marked, condemned, branded. All will shun you, none will love you. You are less than man, less than beast, little more than a thing. You are a violation. Never forget it.

That will be a fine of $37.94. Make sure you move your car for street cleaning next time.

Doing

There's a river I cannot cross,
two palms to each hand,
pleading for a song,
but no tears find me here.

There's a hill I cannot climb,
blinded to dark fragrance,
descended frost covers
my home in fear.

There's a pit I cannot dig,
valleyed depths of hope,
livid stars obscured,
a wild of silent sighs.

There's a place I cannot be,
two sides to a coin not mine,
hide my shadow
where I am not.

These are the things I cannot do,
in whole and form and sum,
weighed and measured.
Now imagine what I can.

Know Your Audience

Dear Mr. Strogatz,

It is with regret that I write to inform you that your work "East of the Grapes of Gatsby" does not suit our needs at this time. This is a highly subjective market, and other publishers may feel differently. I encourage you to persevere in your search, and wish you the best of luck.

This is how I normally would reply, but to do so in your case would be dishonest. Your book is utterly unmarketable. I assure you that it cannot sell a single copy. From now until the end of time not a single person will read it other than your mother, and letting her do so would be one step from matricide. One step worse.

Not only is your work devoid of a fatuous plot, trite characters, or any other device which may recommend it to a busy reader, but it simply cannot hold a candle to the vast array of exciting new releases from which such readers may choose. Classics such as "101 Cat Photos with Captions," "Ungawunga and his/her/their twelve mothers," and "Level Up, Bitches, it be Playin' Time: A guide to Grand Theft Auto 231."

Though I doubt you are capable of improvement, I will offer some specific examples. It takes almost an entire page before the first action scene. Most audiences don't want to wade through almost 200 words of meaningless description, groundwork, and development before a payoff.

Worse, the ending isn't obvious until the end. What audience wants to feel it's in the dark, to be mocked and insulted and proved incompetent? They get that all day everyday in the real world. What readers need is a sense of superiority born from artificial knowledge of a fiction. If they're not smarter than some made-up character, who *are* they smarter than?

Readers want to be able to scream advice at the main character, and many do. "Don't go into that room!" "Kiss her!" "She's a he!" "That's not a cat!" If they wanted to remain ignorant and confused, they'd stick with waking up each morning. If they wanted to be told how stupid they are, they'd listen to their bosses and spouses and children and cats. Readers need to *know*. Something. Anything. It's your job to make them know.

Why is cat 98 cuter than cat 34? Which of Unga-wunga's mothers had her, and which harbor racist thoughts toward the nearby Rmbimbi tribe of which she secretly is a child?

But it's more than this. There is not a single turn of phrase which would appeal to a modern audience. In fact, most are downright offensive. Take for example your absurd opening: "All greatest of times are the same, but in each worst of times there is a madness which makes a woe in its own special way." Anyone who graduated before they stopped teaching grammar can weave such overly florid prose. Nobody wants to read that stuff.

Though linguistically immaculate, your writing is neither compelling nor subtle. You would have done better to attend a modern MFA program, or just read 20,000 nearly identical modern authors. They would have taught you that adroit storytelling on an epic scale is the first folly of children. Do you believe your fiction more compelling than another's reality?

There is no need to resort to such contrivances. Everybody has a story to tell, and it is their own. What right have you to speak of things you've never directly experienced? To invent this or that nonsense, cloak it in verbal roughage, and force it on your unwitting dinner guests? There are two legitimate forms of writing: memoir and narrative. If your story lacks I or me on every line, it should be told by somebody else. It is about him or her or they or it, and only he or she or they or it may tell it.

Here is another example which I found patently offensive: "It is as they said – he inclines, while she declines." You may imagine this to be cute, but it is insulting, offensive, and extremely obnoxious. Do you not understand how much excess thought you have demanded of the reader? Why not adhere to standard modern usage, as specified in the latest MLA guidebook. I'll make an exception to my usual policy, and offer a specific line-edit. "The ho said no." Note the parsimony of language. Four words, none polysyllabic. This is masterful writing.

Your book has another major flaw. It does not courageously regurgitate the consensus political opinion of the literary industry. Instead, you cravenly dodge social issues and activist stances in favor of story-telling and careful construction. This is unacceptable and probably offensive. Why would anybody want to read a book which fails to reinforce their traditionally nontraditional social views?

I also was troubled by your word count. A novel is not supposed to be more than 20,000 words. It is sheer arrogance to suppose that anyone, and I do mean *anyone*, would wish to spend more than three hours with your characters. Three hours is longer than a movie. It's three television episodes, two levels in a video game.

Every hour you steal is an hour which could be spent browsing the web, racking up ad revenue. Your lack of brevity, your incompetence, your ego is stealing money from other books, other sellers. You're not the only game in town. Don't try to hog all the attention. Fortunately, most consumers are too wise for that. They'd never let a shyster like you through the door in the first place.

For the innumerable reasons I've enumerated, you should not only cease submitting your book. You should cease writing books. You should cease thinking about books, except perhaps to read some. Check out our catalog for many excellent titles. And if you, against all advice and reason and decency, decide to continue down this fruitless path, I have a few thousand self-help titles I can offer. At least one of them is bound to make you a better person, by convincing you to stop writing.

Safe

There is a city I have visited which knows no ill.

The women know the men to be brutes and lechers, and the men know the women to be liars and teases. Yet they exist in perfect harmony, hurrying past one another with resentful glance, furtive step, anxious of what he may do, she may say.

On rare occasion, a man hesitates, as if about to speak to a woman or perhaps ask directions. No victim, she points and screams for help, and the vile animal is hauled away before he can terrorize others.

Once in a long while, a woman smiles at a man or perhaps at something behind him. With a look of disgust, the man scowls and calls for help, and the immoral strumpet is hauled away before she can seduce others.

But these are few, the excrement every city produces, however peaceful, however blessed. Most enjoy a quiet existence, each in their own home, causing no harm and receiving none, wondering what it would be like to have someone in their life, and why they never do.

It is a quiet city, and safe.

Bloody Mary

Bloody Mary is an unfair moniker. Why should *she* get all the credit. What about Bloody Elizabeth and Bloody Victoria, and let's not be sexist, Bloody John and Bloody James. For any name there certainly is a Bloody somebody. In fact, there probably are so many Bloody somebodies that it's best just to leave off the title. This is why we now call people by their first names. The title simply is understood.

Ideal

In the diseased state to which we bind ourselves forever willing ever sad, there is no apotheosis that cannot be found by derelict minds in the attic of our conceit.

Poetry Festival

Me, me, me, me, I, I, I, I, here's some more stuff about me and I.

I'm not really a poet so here's a lecture about this thing I'm interested in. People walk away when I talk about this thing I'm interested in, but you can't because you're sitting and the door is closed.

This is a great poem, but all of you know that, because you're all in my poetry group and will cheer for my success in getting to read the same thing to you in a different location.

I didn't really have time during the last six months to prepare for this, so I wrote something on a piece of toilet paper on the way over, but I gave it to a homeless guy who needed toilet paper, and instead I'll read a piece about how I didn't get a chance to prepare. Yeah, meta. There, done.

Somewhere in this disorganized jumble of sheets are a few poems which I couldn't be troubled to find ahead of time, so I'll instead read this poem by someone else I came across in this morning's Times.

I don't really know much about writing or poetry, but wanted a standing ovation anyway, so I wrote about recent events from a perspective with which you are guaranteed to agree, and because we share this political affinity you will feel guilty for not showing solidarity if you do not give me a standing ovation.

I view poetry as a form of healing and catharsis. For me. I have no interest in you or your feelings or your time, so I'll just use the next several minutes as free psychotherapy which, multiplied by the number of audience members, is quite a bargain!

Bad things happened to me, and I'm sure they are much much much worse than the bad things which happened to you, and if bad things didn't happen to you then you come from a place of privilege and plenty and have no right not to appreciate my speaking about the bad things which happened to me, however ineloquently expressed.

Experimental cool brilliant deep profound smart ever-so-smart riveting novel unexpected gimmicky effective, now give me tenure.

This will move you, just like your poem moved me and I cried and applauded so hard when you read, and you'll do the same I know you will understanding how hard it is to be a poet and not know the things which actually would move you to cry and instead just tweet to all our friends about how brilliant you are so you'll do the same for me.

I'm really old and speak with an unmistakably erudite diction, hence you will take my utterances for profundity, my errors for anachronisms, my idiosyncratic manner for the charming style of a bygone era, and my drivel for a mastery which never existed but the usages of age impute to me anyway.

Now, tell me, why can't we get more people interested in poetry?

Instructions

Instructions for orderly disposal of byproducts: Form two lines. Face the person across from you, and point your gun. Only one of you will fire. It is considered proper etiquette for women to fire at men, older to fire at younger. Retrieve your partner's unfired bullet. Step sideways until all gaps have been closed. If you find yourself without a partner, form a pair with the unmatched individual next to you. If you are a sole unpaired individual at either end, remain as you are until the next round. Repeat until no repetition is possible. If you are the last remaining individual, congratulations you are the loser. Please turn off the lights.

I Don't Like Your Face

I don't like your face.

Why don't you like my face?

I'm not quite sure. Can't I just not like it?

Oh no. To just not like it would show no nuance, no discernment. Surely you do not wish to be unnuanced, undiscerning.

It's hard to pin down. I just don't like it.

Think it through. It is important that you know the very reason you don't like it.

Why? Is it not enough that I don't like it? That I don't like something should be all I need know about it.

There are reasons, and there are reasons. Some are allowed, some are not.

Allowed? Who says whether such a thing is allowed or not?

People say. Sometimes the police. Sometimes the people around you. Do you wish for everyone to secretly or not-so-secretly judge you?

I still don't understand why the reason matters. Why would anybody care about my reasons? All they need to know is all I need to know: I don't like your face.

It makes a difference what your reasons are. The reason for a thing is more important than the thing itself. Your reasons are you and you are your reasons.

Well then what sort of reason is acceptable?

If it is because my face it too thin or my left eye is too high, then I suppose that is ok.

You don't mind if I don't like your face as long as this is why? I do not think either of those things are true, though. At least, I did not notice them to be.

But if you don't like it for a wrong reason, then that will not do. You have no right not to like it for a wrong reason. You even could get in trouble.

I'm not sure I quite understand, but I do not wish to get in trouble unless it is trouble I wish to get into. Tell me these wrong reasons, so I make sure I only don't like your face for the right reason.

There are many, and I can't pretend to know them all. Besides, they change day to day, and sometimes moment to moment.

Then give me an example, so I at least know what to look out for.

Well if you don't like the shape of my left eyebrow that would be ok, but if you don't like the shape of my right eyebrow that would be wrong.

Why would that be wrong but not the other?

I'm not entirely sure. Most likely the people with misshapen right eyebrows have a movement and that movement convinced a politician and that politician said that right eyebrow shape was special and protected and anyone who disliked such things wasn't a moral person.

So I should be careful to avoid movements and politicians.

Not at all. That would be silly and pointless and probably illegal. You just need to avoid disliking my face for the reasons they say you shouldn't.

And what if I don't avoid such things. What would happen if I don't like your right eyebrow?

If you don't like the color or texture you'd be fine.

I don't like the shape.

Shhh. Don't say it so loud or you'll get in trouble. If you dislike such things, you're a disliker of such things, and the only people who are dislikers of misshapen right eyebrows are bad people. It's bad to be a bad person or thought to be a bad person.

Why? What will happen?

You may go to jail. At the very least, people will write nasty things about you. Nobody likes a bad person.

I wouldn't be liked? That seems an awful thing, and quite unearned for the simple act of not liking your face.

I don't disagree. But it's not the act of not liking my face that is the problem. It's that you don't like the shape of my right eyebrow. It makes you immoral and wrong and a bad person. Or maybe it just shows that you are.

I don't feel like a bad person. I don't dislike everybody's right eyebrow. Just yours. And your face. But I think it's because of the shape of the right eyebrow. Does that make me a bad person, somebody you don't like?

Well, not you specifically. Just bad people in general. Nobody likes a bad person. Except maybe other bad people. Or the bad person's mother, but probably not.

So nobody likes me?

I'm sure there are parts of you people like. Some people and some parts. Just not the parts that are bad. And maybe not some other parts too.

What parts?

Well I can't speak for everyone, but I don't like your face.

Primitive

The first man who was born thought to himself... nothing because he did not know to think.

He did not know he was the first man born or that he should wonder about where he came from or what he should do or whether it was fiscally responsible to keep interest rates low.

All he knew was that he should eat and screw and poop and sleep.

He was much wiser than modern man.

Doom

There is blood on these hands.

Not real blood you idiot, allegorical blood. Real blood is dangerous. I could get infected. It's certainly not sanitary.

And there will be hell to pay.

Metaphor. Metaphor. Metaphor. I'm not sure what sort of fee hell charges, but it is bound to be hefty. Everyone charges fees these days. That's pretty substantial real estate too, so I'll bet the price is quite high. And then there's the matter of currency conversion. I doubt hell has a good exchange rate.

From the bowels of oblivion.

It's an analogy, dumbass, not actual bowels. I want nothing to do with anything that came out of actual bowels, be they oblivion's or anyone else's. That's just disgusting. Maybe you're into that sort of thing, but you can count me out of your sick little games.

The shadow of things unborn is cleft.

We're talking imagery here, bozo. I don't actually go around cleaving shadows. There's not much point. But if I *was* the sort to go around cleaving shadows, I'm pretty sure it would be harder with things unborn than those walking around and making a nuisance of themselves.

An eternal evisceration of soul and body and mind.

Ah yes, I can see why you may be confused. This one's not allegory or metaphor or analogy or imagery. I've got my tools ready, and eagerly anticipate our appointment.

Interred

Why must I wait until I die to be placed in the soil? That is inefficient, pointless, expensive. I will not enjoy the cool wet decay of the soil if I wait to be put in it. Much better to let it grow around me, a chrysalis in which life becomes death.

Disquisition

This is an inquisitive disquisition on the inquisition. But lest we be peremptorily preempted by a perfunctory prefect, I should note that vigorous exsanguination always is an option should one find oneself at a loss for words.

Say It right

You wish to say something, but can you say it right?

Will your voice be just the right volume, strong but not jarring, soft but not weak. Will it have the right pitch and timbre and grace, an envelope which invites and rebukes and caresses in all the right places and none of the wrong ones.

Will it carry itself with poise, breathing the countless feelings pressed by a will stronger than strong into that tiny place and which must never be allowed free. Will every unintentional crack and cough and throat-clearing carry the absence of intention which itself is intention.

Will it be whimsical yet somber, hold the listener firm until, predation done, the husk is tossed aside, drained of interest. Will it say what needs to be said, how it needs to be said, to whom it needs to be said? Will it do all this absolutely right, but for the most imperceptible of errors? Even these cannot be forgiven.

Think on this. Thinking costs nothing, but saying does not. The consequences are dire and the cost unbearable, or perhaps the consequences are unbearable and the cost dire. It is hard to say, which is one more reason not to.

Why do this to yourself, why go to such lengths? Is it really worth all that? Think long and think hard and then say it. Or do not. What are the chances that all these things will be true, that everything will be just right, that your saying will meet with listening, much less acceptance, much less approval.

In all the universe, of all the ways to say things, of all the things to be said, of all the people to say them to, what are the chances you got it just right?

Best not to say.

Spleen Squeezer

You probably never heard of Spleen Squeezer, but you may owe him your life. Or at least a tiny fraction of your 401K. But don't try to thank him. You won't be able to. His true name is unknown.

Spleen Squeezer appears ordinary to the eye. He is just like you or me, but for his special power. What power does he have? I'll tell you what power he has. It's quite impressive.

He may apply, on rare occasion, an almost imperceptible pressure to the spleen of an adversary. I can see you are skeptical. What use is such a thing? What an unimpressive power. What a useless power. What a laughable power.

It is not. Such a thing is far more troublesome, far more potent than you imagine. He is a hero in the truest sense of the word. Of all the things in this world, of all the happenings, of all the causes and effects and deeds and abilities, there is nothing outside of nature.

Nothing but this one case. This one power. This one ability to cause minor discomfort in an inessential organ. Whether by choice or inability, Spleen Squeezer has never harmed a man, never caused more than the subtlest inconvenience. On occasion, he has helped doctors. But not very often or very much.

I know what you are thinking, and you are wrong. The thing seems trivial until you consider what it truly is. Spleen squeezer represents a violation of the physical order of the universe. The only violation. Why him? Why spleens? Why a violation of everything we know, to such pointless purpose? It almost feels obscene, a mockery, the universe defecating on our reason.

Just as anything may be proven from a single false premise, it may seem anything can be accomplished from a single violation of nature. Don't be absurd. How can we change the universe by squeezing spleens?

What *can* be accomplished is the production of papers and tenure and possibly, if we're very lucky, the discovery of new physics and new chemistry and new biology. Maybe new logic, but we have no way of proving that with old logic.

Instead of spending billions on particle accelerators and telescopes, perhaps we need only study Spleen Squeezer. If he'll allow us. We must be careful with one such as he. None of us wish to offend someone of such power. We could have our spleens squeezed.

Several government agencies proposed weaponizing Spleen Squeezer. Perhaps he could create fusion or a black hole. It was widely suggested he should become an assassin. Surely someone who could squeeze a spleen could pinch a vessel in just the right place. Not so. If he could do that, Spleen

Squeezer would be Vessel Pincher. But he is Spleen Squeezer, nothing more and nothing less.

Naturally, there are some who have tried to kill Spleen Squeezer. It is not that they feared having their spleens squeezed, though there may have been a component of that. Nor were they enemy saboteurs seeking to neutralize our strategic spleen squeezing advantage. Rather, they were scientists.

They realized that the ability to squeeze a spleen was an abomination, a violation. Because of Spleen Squeezer, all we knew was false. But if Spleen Squeezer was no more, then it would be true. All those equations and papers would remain correct, all those hours spent studying and getting grants would not be in vain.

You may think this tale will end with a pun about the attackers being full of spleen, but it does not. It is an elegy, not a comedy. Spleen Squeezer is no more, though not by the agency of man. Perhaps the universe could not abide such a being. The laws of the world can only bend so far before breaking, or snapping back. Or maybe he just didn't watch his step while taking that selfie. Either way, I fear we never shall see the likes of Spleen Squeezer again. Whoever he was.

Disrupted

Do not fear distraction, do not fear interruption. Genius works in its own time, and will brook no impediment.

Have you not heard of the Pandoricon Egregious of Gaius Rubius? None have argued that it isn't the greatest work in any language. Right before committing his seminal idea to paper, his wife pounded on the door of his study demanding that he fix that cart he kept promising to work on.

Have you not heard of Amor Wilson's Principle of the Contraindicative? There is no dispute that it is the grandest yet most tectonic innovation that logic ever has seen. Right before recording his sudden flash of insight, some friends asked him to come drinking.

Have you not heard of Malcolm Tiney's Symphony de Triumpf Magnificat? None who have heard it can suffer to listen to anything else. Right before recording the central motif from his dream, there was a knock on the door from a traveling salesman.

Have you not heard of Shao Le's Theory of Etheric Torsion Displacement? It is impossible to describe the physics revolution ushered in by it. Right before reifying its underpinnings, the phone rang and he was asked for a student recommendation.

Have you not heard of Anne Rudovnikov's Biofoam

▷

Quantistor? One cannot list the technologies it opened to us. Right before she united its improbably disparate parts, her computer beeped an email alert.

Next time you worry that the moment will pass, the opportunity vanish, that now is the only time, calm yourself. Why fret if you know of such grand examples to the contrary?

All You Mean to Me

Let me explain all that you mean to me, the impact you have on my life, how much I care about you.

All that you are, all the thoughts you've thought, all the deeds you've done, all the lovers you've loved, all the hopes you've hoped, these pale in comparison to this thing I feel for you, toward you, about you. The sum total of everything is nothing beside this something you are to me.

It is all I feel, all I need to feel, all I can feel when it comes to you and it encapsulates, summates, obviates everything else about you. This thing cannot be expressed in words, but I will try.

You're blocking my bicycle, get out of my way.

Natural Wonder

Seen one way, our ecosystem is a remarkable confluence of biochemical processes, carefully tuned and coordinated to allow each species a niche, to balance the transformation of biomass between its various forms. Seen another way, we breathe the farts and eat the shit of others, and they of us. There is no dignity in nature, only delusion.

Noticed

I cry out, in this place or that, louder and louder, plead, rant, preach.

Nobody listens, passersby ignore me, not even the police take notice.

I have tried to make myself heard, but have no microphone, no audience, no voice.

Irrelevance is the worst torment, but wouldn't the condemned disagree?

Satisfaction

You have been wronged, and society offers no means of satisfaction. But you have the right to satisfaction, nay the obligation of satisfaction. Who are you to renounce satisfaction, and who are they to refuse it?

If society denies such a thing, you must take it on your own. That simply is the way of things. And society always will deny satisfaction. Those whom it serves already have satisfaction, and those it does not never will. Not by its hand. So you must rely on your own.

Start with the prosecutor, the judge, the lawyer, the CEO of whatever corporation harmed you, the people directly responsible, the people who directly benefited, and the people who simply did not care. Punish them as only you can. As only you must.

They took all you have, lessened you. You must regain this, if such a thing is possible. You must at least repay them in kind. That is what was denied you, and that is what you must take. Why? This is the way of things. Any other way and they will win and you will lose. You will clean their toilets while they sip fine wine and laugh about the sucker, the fool, the nobody.

So you must take what they have. Their homes, their reputations, their families. Yet you still will not have satisfied the needs of satisfaction. Who voted for these people? Who enacted their decisions? Who owns stock in their villainy? Ignorance is no excuse under that law or this. They must pay in kind.

Otherwise, you will clean their toilets and they won't even know who you are or why you are stuck doing so. You will be lessened while they remain content in oblivious impunity. Such a thing cannot be allowed. It violates the law of equivalent exchange.

Begin with the middle managers, the law clerks, the police, the officials large and small, the employees, the functionaries. Work your way through them and their families. Now on to the voters, the shareholders. Is it an excuse that someone's pension held shares in a company which held shares in another? Such arrangements are scribbles on paper, ephemera, fiction. What was done to you was real. There can be no abstraction of responsibility, of guilt. They and their families must pay. You must make them pay.

Once you've worked your way through these, there remain those who sympathized with them. They need not have sympathized on this precise matter. A sympathy is a sympathy, and a sympathizer is a sympathizer. They must not go unpunished. They sympathized with those unworthy of sympathy. Aiding and abetting is a crime under that law and this. You must punish them and their families.

This is difficult work, tedious work, important work. Do not expect it to be quick, do not make it quick. Each must be shown proper attention. You cannot rush such things. Nobody respects a slipshod job. Breathe and focus and excel at every piece of every task. It is no different from climbing a mountain. If you look toward the top, you will be daunted by the enormity of your climb. Look at your feet, and put one in front of the other.

There are more, so many more. What of those who did nothing? They did not know, but they did not trouble to know. They too will pay you no mind as you clean their toilets, as they breeze through their lives. Those lives must not be breezy.

They must know what they did not do, what they should have done. They must rue their negligence. Being witless does not excuse unwitting complicity. You must punish them and their families, working your way outward in ever-expanding circles. Feel free to interrogate, to acquire each new name from the screams and gurgles and pleas of the previous.

Be of good cheer as you do good work. You draw closer to satisfaction. Is not worthy toil the joy of life? You had joy, and they took it. Now you will have it again. A grander joy, that of a job well done, of purpose. Real purpose.

Hum while you work, even sing. It is through such labor that we find true joy. Not the truest joy, just true joy. The truest joy comes later. When one looks upon the vast field of carnage and thinks: this is mine. I wrought this, and all is as it should be.

One day, there will be nobody left. This may happen suddenly, unexpectedly. You lift the scythe, and realize all the wheat has been cut. There remains nobody but you. Breathe deep. You have done it.

You have received satisfaction. You have wrested it from a world bent on denying you, disdaining you, ignoring you. Now you may move forward with your life, and none shall impede you. There are no toilets left to clean, and you no longer are pathetic, contemptible, weak. You are somebody again. If you are unsure, look around. You must be somebody. There is nobody else.

You feel a qualm, the subtlest hint of dissatisfaction. This is natural. It is the release of a struggle won, the self-doubt of a kingdom conquered. You have nobody to govern, nobody to judge you. Nobody but one. One problem.

What part did *that* person play in your downfall? What did you do to you? Don't act innocent. Your own judgment was deferred, as was your punishment. You already lost everything, have no family or reputation or possessions. But this does not mean you have nothing.

You gained something through your toil. You gained satisfaction. You must take from yourself all that you have. Begin with your satisfaction, end with your life.

There. Now you are done, with justice and satisfaction meted out in due proportion to all. The world is as it should be. It is satisfied.

Righteous

To the crusader there only is the crusade, and the entire world is seen through its lens. He cares nothing for you or your family or the things you hold dear unless they happen to agree with his crusade, in which case you too are a crusader or a follower or a sympathizer and soon-to-be convert.

There only ever has been one crusade, but past men were too foolish to recognize it. They were led astray by faux crusades of their own. The epic battle is culminating now, at the precise moment the crusader is crusading. The deeds of his crusade will echo for aeons. There can be no future crusade, no other crusade. *His* crusade will remove the need. It will succeed, banish the foe, bring light to a world darkened by the crimes of others.

It is best to be the crusader. His cause is pure and immutable. He harbors no doubt, only a small but perfect knowledge of what must be. How he came by this knowledge is irrelevant. It is right, and no more need be said. The crusader is happy, as the righteous always are.

It is best not to be the crusadee, or the one who seeks to convince the crusader or infect his resolve with nuance, or the one who intentionally stands in his way or accidentally stands in his way or stands nearby or lives in the world his crusade creates. In fact, it is best not to coexist in the same time and place with the crusader.

But there exists a crusader in every time and place, and he always is right. You must be him to be happy.

Latinate

I'd like to speak Latin. Not learn it, just speak it. Everything sounds impressive in Latin, dumb in English. If I knew Latin, then I would sound smart. And sounding smart is half of being smart.

You agree don't you? You're half smart, though I think you got the wrong half. If you had my half, you wouldn't be here. You would be listening to someone sounding smart in Latin. Not me sounding dumb in English. I'll show you what I mean. Listen carefully.

"I wonder what these tools are for? They have such odd shapes."

See, sounds stupid in English. But in Latin... well, I don't know what it is but I'll bet it sounds good. Here, now you try one. Oh, I see. That was rude of me. Ok, I'll do it for you.

"Please give me back the parts I need to speak."

Well that was quite a mouthful, but I'll bet it would sound a lot better in Latin. You should thank me. You're lucky you no longer have those parts. You don't have to worry about sounding stupid. You get to keep the half of being smart which isn't sounding smart. The half which couldn't keep you from ending up here. Or is it ending here? I'll bet the difference would be clear in Latin.

Well, let's get on with it. No, no, not the examples.
I've said my fill about Latin, just not *in* Latin. It's a
mere fancy of mine, an idle wish. I mean, who has
time to learn Latin when there's so much else to do?
Like figure out what to do with these curious tools.

But I'm being rude. I assumed you don't know Latin.
Do you know Latin? Feel free to show me up. I don't
hold a grudge. We've got plenty of time, and maybe
I'll even pick up a little Latin along the way.

Direction

My suggestion, my earnest deep-down, bottom-of-the-heart suggestion, is to go away. Going away is the right answer, it's not the wrong answer, and definitely not the wishy-washy answer. It means you're doing something, improving your existence, because all moving-forward is progress. You're a progressive, progressing your way in this direction or that. It matters not. The point is progress. And going away. Specifically, going away from me. I'm bad for you, very bad, so bad that you shouldn't be anywhere near me, or even think of being anywhere near me. But going away will solve that. Why don't I go away? I already did. I'm away. This is my away. You need to find your own. We each only get one, even if we imagine there are many aways and do-overs or that we each meander on some long path intersecting and bifurcating at the whim of the universe. That's nonsense. That's weak. That's not going away, it's just going. This is different. This is taking control of your life. You're not doing what the universe, which you're a part of but delude yourself into thinking you're not, says. You're not doing what anyone says. Least of all somebody no good for you like me. I can't tell you to go away, can't make you go away. Only you can do that. And you should. Far far away. To that place. Away. Where you're not you and nobody else is you and nobody even knows you or knows at all or can know or maybe would want to know. You can reinvent yourself as not you or nothing at all. Away. But you only get to do it once. So choose well. Pick an away you'll want to go

to, where you won't be bothered by noisome people
who you think should go away. Otherwise, you'll
spend all your time advising them to do what's best,
what's wisest. To go away.

Object of Hatred

Somewhere in this room is an object that wishes to kill you.

No, I didn't plant it. There's no boobytrap. If there is, it's not mine. Yet somewhere in this room is an object that wishes to kill you.

This object's sole purpose, its raison d'etre, its hope and joy is to kill you. It hates you. Unconditionally, viscerally, and untainted by reason or cause. That's just the way it is.

Maybe its fibers were woven a certain, secret way — if it has fibers, which it may or may not. Or maybe it absorbed the soul of a violent psychopath intent on murdering someone with your middle initial, your eyelashes. Perhaps magic words were spoken over it by a bitter old witch you inadvertently slighted in the supermarket checkout line. Or maybe it just doesn't like your taste in hats. I can't say, and I don't know.

Such purity of hatred is beautiful. How many things in this world do we know to be pure? Pure things would have no traffic with such as you and I. Except one. This would have traffic with you. And will.

Don't try to guess which object it is. You won't be able to. The cursed object looks like all the rest. Maybe the rest are cursed too, but I doubt it. What are the odds of two such pure objects in the world, let alone in the same room and with the same purpose? So let's just say it is one. That is a safe assumption. Safe for me.

If it is more than one, you may find out the hard way. But there is no reason to despair. I doubt you stand a chance against even one cursed object. The difference between none and one is far greater than the difference between one and many. It is the difference between being unhated and hated. Between me and you. What matters the degree, the number of knives which seek your blood? Probably not literal knives, though. That would be gauche.

Your purpose is to stay alive, to not be killed by the cursed object. Perhaps that chair's purpose is to extinguish you. Or maybe it's just a comfortable place to sit. It is hard to tell. The only way to find out is to find out, and that could be most unfortunate for you.

Do you even know what qualifies as an object? Does the clock on the wall count, or its dial, or its hands? Maybe the color of the dial is the object, or the concept of a clock. Maybe it is the air you breathe, or a speck of dust in it. You just need to avoid that particular speck. Can you? Maybe it already settled on you, inaugurating your corruption.

What will the object do? I wonder the same thing. I never have seen a cursed object in action. It would be interesting to see, but that does not mean I wish you ill. I am not the cursed object, or maybe I am and do not realize it. There is no use speculating.

How do I know all this? I deduce, I intuit, I sense. It is all I can do. I wish I could help, be more specific, guide you in finding or avoiding this thing. But I am limited. Just like you, except for this thing or that. Things like knowing something in this room is filled with hate. That this hate is pure and specific. That you are its object.

Cost

What are you whining about, complaining to him and her and everyone who will listen. Which is nobody who matters.

So you're living in the street, broke, bankrupt, homeless, destitute. Isn't everybody these days? Look at the bright side. If you had something, you'd have to lose it before you'd be living in the street, broke, bankrupt, homeless, destitute. Before you'd have a place, a status, a condition. Before you'd be eligible for the million benefits our benign and enlightened society offers to those with that place, status, condition.

What's that? You had a nice job and a home and a family, and everything was taken away? Well, that's not really fair is it. It wasn't taken away. You gave it away, traded it for things you wanted. Like a college education or medical treatment or elbow wax. That's your fault, and no other's. It speaks to poor fiscal management.

I think you're confused. Sure, a college education costs a billion dollars, a doctor's appointment a trillion, an elbow wax a quadrillion. But you can't expect an enlightened society to give handouts to people with a nice job and a home and a family. Don't be so selfish. There's only enough for those living in the street, broke, bankrupt, homeless, destitute. Which you are. Now. So cheer up. You qualify.

All those things which were so expensive now are free for you. You just had to rid yourself of that pesky life, get dragged into the muck and abyss like the rest of us. Quite frankly, I don't know why you're so bitter about losing your nice job and home and family. They were impediments. They kept you from qualifying.

You don't need to worry about any of that anymore. You're here. Now you too can line up for soup, spend your days scrounging in the gutter, digging through trash. Just like everyone else. And I do mean everyone else.

Welcome to today, my friend. It's the beginning of the rest of your life.

UBeU

They'll tell you to be yourself, be true to yourself, follow your muse. That the world will accept and applaud and admire you for being yourself.

Don't believe them. Be that other guy instead. The one who is rich and successful and has everything he wants. He's not unhappy, shallow, or lonely. But you will be. If you listen to them.

Do you accept and applaud and admire everyone else? They are being themselves. Who else could they be? They took this advice. The ones you do accept and applaud and admire are the ones who did not.

Ask yourself who gives such advice. Is it misery or success which loves company? In a small world filled with a great many people, would they really want to share? Best to deceive the competition, thwart it.

They'll say it is talent not work which makes you. Don't study hard, just let your inner beauty express itself. How much inner beauty do you see expressing itself? For inspiration, look to the works of great artists who never were.

Follow your heart and it will lead you down the path you were meant to follow. Do you want to follow the path you were meant to follow? We all are meant to die. The last path you should follow is the one you were meant to. What are the odds the universe loves you? Your path will lead to the same dismal place as everyone else's. Buy a lottery ticket if you think you are special.

Even if they mean well, who are you listening to? If they know so much why aren't they following their own advice. If they are, and this advice is their art then you can see how poorly it turned out. Do you wish everyone to see such inner beauty? It is indecent and personal and quite unpleasant to look at.

Ask yourself to whom they give such advice. Is it to you and you alone, confidentially whispered in your ear? Or is it spoken aloud, screamed by the incontinent at anyone and everyone. Please, please listen, that we may drag you down. To be like us. Then our failure won't be ours. It will be yours too.

Is it your particular genius, you being you, you being true to yourself, your muse which they accepted and applauded and admired? If so, what need have you of advice. You already are recognized for being you. You already are accepted and applauded and admired.

Do they wish to help introduce your greatness to the world, interpret it for them? Or is it tired words regurgitated by tired mouths to any foolish enough to pay heed.

If they tell you to be yourself, do not listen. The world has no room for one such as you. It will ignore or despise or destroy you. Be someone else instead. Someone it *will* accept and applaud and admire. To do this is easy. All you need to know is that the world has very bad taste.

Sentimentality

It is an evocative sentiment, one which evokes, provokes, invokes. Not in some trite, smarmy, and over-sentimentally self-indulgent sense. But in the old sense, the real sense. Balial and Metr'shiva and Kash-klinnan and a dozen other names long forgotten and best forgotten but now evoked and provoked and invoked. Look what you've done with your sentiment. Now, we all will have to suffer for it.

Dotage

"A country may be so bound by procedure and form that it cannot choose the path of right, even if it knows it and fervently desires to do so. Such a country is an empty vessel, its people stumbling into the void. Arms tied and eyes covered, they are powerless, however great their strength, however acute their sight. Such a nation has entered its dotage. However venerable it once may have been, it no longer can hold the spoon with which to feed the conscience of its citizens."

— *Last words of Arthur the Indiscreet before his execution for Offense.*

Pep

You've already heard several rousing speeches, and you will hear several more before the day is done. Like my colleagues, I welcome you to our family, our team, our noble pursuit. However, I lack their gilded words. My own love of the Party is strong, perhaps stronger still for this lack of gilded words.

My words will be simple but real. Feel them in your hearts and you will do well. They are stern words for a stern world, and it is only because I know you are of great spirit, handpicked by the Leader himself, that I thus enjoin you.

You may feel you have made it. Do not. None of us has made it. The Party is Parent. The Party is Priest. But the Party is constantly under threat. You must do what you can to defend it, advance it, and bring freedom and purity to the rest of the world.

This is not easy. It will take work. Are you ready for it? We shall see. I look at you and see softness, weakness, potential greatness. You must be ready with discipline, diligence, and an indomitable spirit.

When Vlad decided to kill 24,000 prisoners in 1462, did his executioner complain? Whinge about having to do so much work, cut so many trees, sharpen so many stakes, tie and impale so many writhing, screaming men? No, he hunkered down and set to work. There were no factories, no armies of functionaries to assist. He and a couple of helpers went to it. Heaven knows what they had to endure and how long it took. They did it because it was their duty.

When Basil II defeated the army of Samuel in 1014, he ordered the entire captured army of 15,000 blinded. This was 30,000 eyes minus one he left to each 100th man. Do you have any idea how much work that was? A poker had to be heated and then held near each eye until it melted. That took time and patience. Were there a thousand executioners? Of course not. It was one or two dedicated individuals, once again proving that individual excellence advances and ennobles any cause. Heating the irons, holding the panicking soldiers, melting the eyes, disposing of the fluids must have seemed an insurmountable task. Yet this is just a single example of what these extraordinary individuals accomplished. They did not boast or complain. They did it because it was their duty.

When Stalin ordered the execution of 7,000 Polish officers at Katyn, a single man managed the deed. Did Mikhailovich Blokhin groan and complain and delay? Did he demand reasonable work days with benefits? Did he automate the process or pawn off the work on subordinates, of which he had plenty? No, he personally administered each shot with dedication and skill. All night, every night for 28 days. This was just a small part of a long and illustrious career doing such things. He even brought his own supply of pistols in case those provided were inadequate. He did not seek reimbursement, or claim disability for repetitive stress syndrome. This was a man who understood the importance of taking responsibility, of doing the job right. He did it because it was his duty.

I won't lie. The task before us is enormous. These achievements, impressive as they sound, pale in comparison. But there are many of us. You are not alone. You will have subordinates and factories and all the resources of the Party. There will be times you feel overworked, overwhelmed, overwrought. At such times, your soul will be revealed. The traitor's soul blames the Party, blames the good, blames the great. The loyal soul finds fault in itself, realizes it is not pure enough, strong enough. The great soul becomes pure enough, strong enough.

At such times you may need something to aspire to. The greatness of our Leader is an inspiration to us all, but not something we can hope to achieve. It would be delusional to try. None can aspire to such heights, nor should they. That place is occupied by the only one who could or should occupy it. Instead, we must look to more accessible examples. Fortunately, we need not look far. The 20th century furnishes many.

The Germans, the Russians, the Cambodians, the Chinese. They knew discipline, they knew diligence, and they discovered their own indomitable spirit. Do you have any idea how hard it is to kill fifty million people? The transport and executions and disposal. Think about it, and think hard. The enormity of such deeds should not be elided. Do you think those workers whined? Demanded overtime? Passed the buck to their juniors? They did what needed to be done. Day in, day out, in long shifts and under terrible working conditions. But they did it anyway. They did it because it was their duty.

So when things get tough, and you begin to question and fear and the darkness creeps in, just remember the ones who came before. Not heroes, not warriors, but workers. It is the workers who make the Party great. And what do workers do? They work. Without complaint or demand or worry. They do what needs to be done, they do what they are called upon to do. Laziness is another word for treason, and there is no I in Party. Great deeds are afoot, and you have the opportunity — nay, the duty — to be an integral part of them.

Party is Parent. Party is Priest. Now get ready to work. We've got a lot for you to do.

Sagely

Simple Drimple was his name
All his words were one and same
Each and every told a lie
He was first among the wise.

Plants

There is something special about a plant. A little bit of green in a dull, drab, nondescript world. A friend you can sniff and smell and run your hand over. It is magical, and refreshing, and can fill the million tiny holes in your soul. There is something special about a plant. What else takes so long to die, quietly letting you watch.

Trash Talk

*Excerpt from the seminal work 'The Proper Ways to Die'
by R. Vandibus Mural*

When I see people pick up after others, it disgusts me. Not the litter or the litterers, but those collecting it. I wish to spit on them, but spitting in public would be as bad as littering. The litterers are not human, cannot be judged by human standards. But these people are, or aspire to be.

What message does it sent? What passive-aggressive weakness is this? If you litter we will clean it for you, for free, at your convenience. We are lower than the trash you wantonly abandon. Please use us, please despise us, we thrive on your contempt.

Do they imagine the litterers will be shamed, see the error of their ways? Such creatures know no shame, have no shame. They cannot be taught or reasoned with. They are things, and must be treated as such.

If you are human, speak up. Strike them in the face. Hard. Force them to clean, repent, behave. Strike them again and again until they do so or are destroyed. Either will do. If you lack strength or courage enough for this, call upon your betters, the strong arm of society. If you lack the clout to do this, what good are you?

It generally is frowned upon to properly punish litterers. Do not let this deter you! Society often mistakes them for its own. Be careful or *you* will be hunted. A human does not fear this, does what he must. If you cannot strike them down, cleanse them, instruct them, there are other ways. Ways which involve their family or pets or prized collection of autographed toilet bowls. Feel no guilt in this. The children and pets and things of nonhumans are nonhuman too.

This is the way to treat litter, and the same principle applies to all else. Do not complain or try to set an example or work to fix the problems others create. They only will create more and care less. Both humans and nonhumans learn through punishment. The difference is that humans are thus educated, nonhumans thus trained.

Those who clean up after others are less than nonhuman. They are less than the trash they clean. They are humans who have forgotten what they are. What farmer serves his pigs?

A Crying Shame

You heard what happened to Jimmy right?

Why, what happened to Jimmy? I thought he was doing well. His store was expanding and his wife is expecting.

He got pinched for the business with that Vira chick?

Vira?

You know, the little girl who drank that stuff.

Oh god, that was some nasty business. A crying shame.

A real tragedy. Something like that happens, you know there's gonna be inquiries.

But wasn't it her fault?

She was a little girl, for chrissake. Nice way to blame the victim. Anyway, somebody was gonna pay.

I suppose so. But what did Jimmy have to do with it?

Oh nothing. He didn't even know her.

I don't get it.

Well, he was the one they picked.

What about the mom?

Are you SERIOUS? What sort of sicko is gonna blame the grieving mom?

But wasn't it an accident?

No such thing. Somebody's always at fault.

But why Jimmy? What about the company that produced the stuff?

I like it. You're thinking like an old-style American. But you know how it works now. Much fairer.

I never really paid much attention to this stuff. Legal mumbo jumbo.

You know, they have to blame somebody. The only fair way is a lottery.

How does that solve anything?

Well, it gives you somebody to blame.

But what *about* the company?

C'mon, you know that's not right. Big company like that is gonna end up being liable for everything. Could sink the economy.

But a random person?

Better than a non-random one. Most nasty stuff happens

to poor people, minorities. If you just look around and blame one of them well, that's downright racist. Or classist. Or some sort of -ist. I forget.

Then why blame anybody? It was just an accident. Bad stuff happens.

And somebody has to be to blame for it. In the old days, they'd have to dig and dig and find somebody who, with perfect foresight, clarity of thought, and expertise would have made a slightly different decision. But that took lots of work. And it always ended up landing on the shoulders of some big corporation or some poor schmo.

Sounds like Jimmy is the poor schmo.

Not poor, the way you tell it. See, the system's working. Fair.

But a guy with an expectant wife?

Can't discriminate. That would be wrong.

Still, it's a crying shame.

A real tragedy.

Walking

It is important to remember that every person walking toward you also will walk away from you. That is the nature of walking.

Fallen

Where will you go, now that you have fallen?

Where is there to go?

It is true. For one who has fallen, there is nowhere.

You are mistaken. There is only one place I can be, and I am there.

Then you have not fallen. The world fell around you.

Sound of Silence

You should puncture your eardrums.

To be safe, you should remove them altogether. Maybe even the piece of brain by which you hear, the entire pathway by which you know of the existence of sound.

I can do this for you. I'm not a doctor, but I have a fork somewhere. Other kitchen utensils too. Let me know if you'd like me to.

Why, you ask? That's part of the problem. You asked, and I'll answer. If you hear this answer it may be too late. The answer may itself be the reason.

There is a sound, some simple combination of tones, which will cause you unspeakable, unending anguish. Another sound will cause elation, happiness, fulfillment. Maybe they are the same sound. It's hard to tell, and then it's too late.

You do not need to hear these sounds. Elation, happiness, fulfillment, and anguish can be had without a devil's bargain. They can be found in this world on their own, piecemeal or together, without sound.

Sounds are too dangerous. There is a sound which will make you immortal, or tell you how. Another will inform you of the future or the past, of your failures, all of them. And there are so many. Yet another can convince you to take a cheese grater to your skin.

All of these sounds, all of these possibilities. Who would have imagined the squawking of monkeys could be so telling, so deadly.

I know what you are thinking. If sound can do all these things to you, maybe you can use sound to do them to another. It is a noble thought, and I encourage you to try. I suggested you puncture your eardrums, not cut out your tongue. Don't put words in my mouth, and certainly don't put any in my ear.

Paradise

The true story of the garden of eden is more mundane than the cautionary fable purveyed by modern religions. The whole bit with the trees and serpent was true enough, but the big guy was a forgiving sort. He never would evict tenants for such a minor infraction. Besides, it was hard to find good ones. But it wouldn't be reasonable to expect him to subsidize their lifestyle indefinitely. During the real estate boom, he sold to a developer. Adam, Eve, and their progeny were relocated to a less desirable, but more affordable location nearby. Rumor has it a wave of gentrification followed, though the area appears to have taken a bit of a downturn lately. As for the flaming sword, it was used to provide suitable illumination during the move in compliance with local safety regulations. After several later incidents of unintended combustion, it was deemed uninsurable and tossed in a lake, where some kid subsequently found it and made some mischief. The moral of the story is don't rent, always buy.

Thirsty

I'm really really thirsty. Did you ever wonder just what's in your water? No, no, I don't know anything specific. I'm just asking. Because, you know, if it was my water I'd be concerned. I mean, you're what percent water? So whatever's in your water ends up in you. Ends up as you. I'm just saying. If it was my water, I'd be extra careful. Do you want to end up as some random chemical? I once did, and let me tell you it's no fun. I almost entirely became some contaminant. Do you want to spend your days as a contaminant? But look at me now. I watch my water. In fact, I'm so cautious, I don't even drink water. Or beer or milk or soda or a seven molar solution of hydrofluoric acid. Nothing with water in it. Because who knows what's in the water that's in the thing. Bet you didn't think of that. It's not just the water, but the stuff containing the water. Like people. Don't drink those either. They contain water, and who knows what's in that water. You *do* know what's in the water? And you drink it anyway? Jeez, that's nasty. But I suppose it's ok then. If I know what's in the water I can drink it. Or a thing containing it. Now I know what's in the water you drank, so I know what's in you. I'm really really thirsty.

Playmate

I won't say you shouldn't play with them per se, but keep in mind that they always turn on you. It may be the first time they encounter you, it may be thirty seven years, six months, three days and twelve hours later at a family barbecue, both awkward and utterly unanticipated.

There will be no warning. If there are signs, they will fall beneath your perception. Perhaps that is why they turn on you, because you cannot perceive what they wish you to perceive, assume you can perceive, demand that you perceive. It may be here or there, sooner or later. But they will turn on you. And when they do, there is no telling what will happen.

All that is certain is that it will be an unpleasant affair. Imagine a thing which loathes you, not because of anything you did or said or didn't do or didn't say. They loathe you because you are, they loathe you to the very core. Every fiber of your being disgusts them, every action offends them. It is not enough to avoid you, forget about you, pretend you do not exist. They cannot do so. Your very existence is anathema to them.

Do not seek cause or effect. Maybe it was not always this way, or maybe it was. Maybe they were dissembling, or maybe they did not know you offended them, unable to place the source of dull throbbing discontent, until they could. Maybe they will act right away, or maybe they first must become certain, muster the courage. Scientists are unsure.

Only one thing is clear: there is no going back. It was not a transition, a gradual shift in awareness or perception or feeling. You did not one day change and become repugnant to them. You always were that way. You must have been. No other explanation is possible to them, no other explanation is acceptable to them.

They simply did not realize what you were or, realizing, act on it. But then they do. At the worst possible moment. The moment you least expect it. A moment you are perfectly comfortable around them, guard down, oblivious to danger.

When they strike, they strike hard. Maybe it is fatal, maybe not. You may wish it was. There is no venom of greater potency, none which causes such pain, none which rots flesh and self so unflinchingly. Without an ounce of regret. Without a shred of mercy.

Be careful. Be very careful. There can be no reasoning, no reconciliation, no hope. They are not what you thought, and never will be. They have turned on you. A dog which once bites its owner must be put down. But you cannot put them down, cannot sever that bond. So you let them go.

They will not forget. All their memories now are tempered with hate. You are the enemy, the thing which ensnared them, tricked them, constrained them all this time. Everything they hate is you, and

you are all they hate. Of hate they have an unlimited
reservoir. Where it comes from is a mystery, but
there can be no doubt of its presence now. Perhaps
it once was love. All it takes is an ounce of hate in a
gallon of love.

At this point, do not hesitate, do not hope. Do what
must be done. And there only is one thing which can
be done. It is a simple thing, an obvious thing: do not
play with them in the first place. They always turn
on you.

Luminary

Ignore the blood on my hands. What I have to say comes from a place of love, is universal, holy, of great substance. It will ennoble, enlighten. My words scream the wisdom of tolerance and kindness for those who deserve the wisdom of tolerance and kindness. You'll know them because I haven't murdered them. But never mind that, I'm the great advocate for great freedom. Your advocate. Their advocate. What I have to say is far more important than the body parts necessary to say it or whom they came from. So praise me, pour your accolades on me, the voice of your generation of your people of you. A professorship, a book deal, political office. None of these will lessen my thirst in service of the cause. Or the blood on my hands. But ignore that. They were random people and random people are less important than my cause, than your cause, than *the* cause. Because there only ever was is or can be one cause. And while it can be advanced by those with no blood on their hands, it somehow never is. So ignore the blood on my hands. It isn't yours. Yet.

Pulpit

Blessed are the meek, because well, they suck and are easy to snack on and frankly don't have the balls to get mad at me for saying they're a bunch of passive aggressive little shits. So they're blessed, and will continue to be blessed all the way into my blessed oven. Praise be to god for the bounty of the earth. Thanks for all the tender meat.

Keep it to Yourself

My voice echoes across recess, cloven wind, an emetic for solitude, deafening my heart.

Fill the hollow with voided hope, an ineluctable residue, creeping stain.

Who ruins sacred silence, vomits into the abyss between us, seeks to communicate at me?

I am incommunicable, incommunal.

Shouting Woman

Today I saw a shouting woman. She was not screaming or bawling or crying or pleading. She was shouting. Her words were ordinary, even mundane. Nor did hysteria hang on her, as one would suppose of a shouting woman.

In all but this one thing, she was perfectly normal. She simply shouted. Every word she spoke was shouted, the tone and intonation and pitch incongruous with meaning. Others tried to ignore her, but found it difficult. Because she was shouting.

Her companion listened patiently, as if oblivious, as if it were the most normal thing in the world. She did not shout back or even raise her voice. If anything she took care to speak softly. It was hard to discern her words, tuned as I was to the shouting.

Perhaps the shouting made her acutely aware of her own voice, of how it carried. Or perhaps she wished to accentuate the contrast, broadcast her own comparable virtue.

No doubt she inwardly cringed. What if she were mistaken for her companion? What if others did not distinguish? What if she became like her, became her, was her. Maybe it was too late, but my eyes were not trained to discern the parts of such a being.

The shouting woman kept shouting. She either did not know or did not care. Maybe she wondered why nobody sat near her. Maybe she shouted so nobody would.

Insignificant Other

It is best to be with someone who represents everything you cannot stand.

What a horrid thing to say, you declare! What a
horrid thing to think! What a horrid person to think
it!

It is just as you say, and just as I hope.

When you are with one who agrees with you and
with whom you agree, who is agreeable to you
and you to them, you are not loved. He loves the
ideal you represent, the group you are part of. Your
position is tenuous, and you will fall in an instant.
When you disagree in the slightest with that ideal,
degrade yourself by the smallest deviation, you
become nothing to him. Another must take your
place. Another untainted by individuality, by the
prosaic flaws of prosaic reality. He loves the general
of which you are one irrelevant particular. You
can do naught but displease him. There is no you,
nowhere to go but down.

Is it not better to be with one who detests your group,
your beliefs, everything about you except you? Who
loves you and respects you and admires you despite
all these things. He hates the general but loves the
particular. Nothing you do can fail him, nothing you
do can deter him. There only is you, nowhere to go
but up.

You wrinkle your nose, your eyes spit contempt. That is absurd and offensive and possibly illegal, you proclaim in utter disgust. But you know I am right, and despise me for it.

We should be perfect for one another. By being so wrong I am right. I hate everything you stand for, everything which matters to you, everything you aspire to. Even though I've never met you. If I did, perhaps I would love you despite hating everything you stand for, everything which matters to you, everything you aspire to. It is a small 'perhaps,' an infinitesimal 'perhaps.' Yet the smallest seed can birth the greatest happiness. Most die instead.

If this seed germinates, you will have what so few ever do. You will be loved. Truly. But unrequited love has no point, is nothing more than a nuisance. You must love me too. Truly. True love can be had only one way, and now you know this way. The best you can do is hope, but such hope is not unfounded. Surely I represent everything you can't stand.

Histories

The benefit of studying history is not to avoid repeating its mistakes. Those who study rarely are in a position to make such mistakes, let alone repeat them. Others will do that, others who never studied history, could not, or would not, and probably should not. They have strong voices and good hair and are eminently qualified to make mistakes.

Don't worry, such mistakes are out of copyright. There is no legal liability in repeating them, so set your mind at ease. But we digress. Not I, just you. If you had listened linearly I would have gotten to the point by now.

The benefit of studying history is to give context. To place the depredations of today on a meaningful scale, to give them units, anchor them amongst their peers.

It is so when something is done or said, you can gauge whether such a thing is worse or better than the million other stupid or harmful or dangerous things which were done or said.

It is so when you are surrounded by fools, drowning in the rank odor of a world of wasted and useless flesh, you know it ever has been this way and only the details changed from time to time.

It is so you realize yourself the only voice of reason, the light, the way. A dumb voice, a dim light, an untrod way.

It is so you understand how alone you are, that in any period only a few truly exist and they never meet and each is completely, utterly isolated. Surrounded with filth and slime and scum, the offal of a world long abandoned by even the illusion of piety and certainly devoid of anything to be pious about. A world which never possessed reason, except through those few isolated ones. Like you. And you don't count.

It is so when you look around and see what you see, you know that it is what you would have seen, modulo a few particulars, anywhere or anytime else.

It is so you know that however bad it gets, it always can get worse. And it will.

It is so you take a deep breath and put things in context. It's not so bad. The lies and hypocrisy and stupidity and cruelty are natural, normal, integral. Nothing's so terrible. You are a brief flame in a dark world. A very very brief flame. In a very very dark world. Life is too short and unpleasant to dwell on how short and unpleasant it is.

It is so you can refuse the world, refuse to let it absorb you more than it already has, refuse to be contaminated and drawn in and down.

It is so you won't spend your very brief time obsessed with things you neither can change nor should. Better to spend it obsessed with trivial things, distracting things, things better suited to your station as an irrelevance.

It is so you see how lucky you are. Other than a brief, unexplained stay utterly alone in a world devoid of meaning, which you never will understand, have no influence on, and at best won't actively destroy you before your time, things aren't so bad. At least you now can put that in context. What you're experiencing is normal. It's what everybody experiences, before they cease to experience.

So quit your bellyaching. Smile and say grace and eat what the world dishes out. You won't have to do it for long.

Doing Good

I've never believed what I was told, I'm a rebel you see, a freethinker. Don't trust authority, my mother once said. I didn't believe her, so I trust authority.

The problem is they don't trust me. It's all because of one or two small misunderstandings. But they're good guys and mean well.

Whenever I look in mirrors, I try to catch my reflection misbehaving. If there's an infinite line of reflections, one of them must slack off at some point. What are the odds they all can mock me perfectly whenever I look?

You may have read about me. It's important not to believe everything you read. My mother told me that, but she probably was lying.

Once at a fair, I had my portrait done. It actually looked like me, but the expression was wrong. How can you paint me *now* when you only saw me *then*, I asked? But he had moved on to the next customer. I visited his tent later to see if his expression would change.

The problem with people is they are inconstant. Their wants never are the same. You ask if they want to live, and they say yes. You offer to take their kid instead, and they say no. A person should know if they want to live. It seems a very basic thing. But I'm a pushover. In the end, I do the extra work. All because they can't decide. I know it's generous of me, yet nobody seems happy. Nobody seems grateful. But that's life. You do your best and everyone complains.

Sometimes I wonder if everything I've been told is a lie, right down to the basics. Could I fly if I wanted to? Gravity seems pretty strong, but I've met some pretty strong guys, and they cried like the rest. Maybe strength is just a word.

I wonder if I'm too heavy to fly. Maybe all the lies weigh me down, constrain me. I'm not sure whether gravity is against me. Maybe it's secretly a friend, an admirer.

Like that reporter who followed me. Why else would she follow me? It's nice to have a secret admirer. I was sad when it wasn't a secret anymore. She must have been full of lies, because she couldn't fly.

It's hard to find people that are pure, that the system hasn't gotten its hands on. Don't get me wrong. Authority is good. I believe in authority. But sometimes it is a hindrance. Sometimes it just doesn't understand. Authority doesn't believe in me.

Like a parent. But it will come around once it sees what I've accomplished. Once it sees that I wasn't just talk or play or wind. Once it sees the good I did. And I *do* good, lots of good.

I'm going to do some right now. You'll see. So let's get started. There's so much good to do. I sure hope you aren't full of lies.

Game of Go

Struggle to
surround,
control,
destroy
a same other
in this
tiny territory
always bound,
action and thought
closely circumscribed
by words written
many years ago,
never looking beyond
for other worlds to
surround,
control,
destroy.

Hush Now

Do not vote, do not write, do not speak!

You may be tempted to complain or challenge or inform or change. Let others be fool enough to do such things. They will not survive, they will not endure.

You shelter alone beneath a rock, hoping to avoid notice, to avoid detection, to avoid.

All the while the rumbles and screams and ramblings of a great insane ape echo in your ears. It flails about in this direction or that, motion from pure emotion, absent meaning, wisdom, and wit.

It moves wildly: heedless, inconstant, and utterly without form or purpose. Covering every inch of its skin are blades and barbs. Any contact will ruin, mutilate, or kill. If you live, you will wish you had not.

The insane ape cannot be reasoned with, predicted, guided. There are those who seek to do so, believe they can do so, die trying to do so. The ape lacks memory and reason. How can one speak sense to such a thing? Some who try become the blades and barbs, tearing the hapless until they in turn are raked off by furious claws.

If one could guide the ape's madness, what then? Today's rebel is tomorrow's hero is the next day's villain. There is no hope in madness, no end or cycle or progress, no redemption or cure or enlightenment. Each work is undone by the next. Even this is uncertain, for there can be no certainty in unseeing delirium.

The ape is the size of a mountain, a mountain of mountains. Best to hide as it meanders aimlessly across the landscape, its only legacy ruin. Best to hope you remain unnoticed or at least unremarked.

The most you can do is try to avoid the insane ape, keep out of its way, and live a quiet life. Better to be trampled unseen than be seen and lessened. The insane ape does not wish to harm you or not harm you, but it will. It is not angry or sad or loving. Or maybe it is all those things at once and never. Who knows how the ape thinks, what it will do? Best to stay away, keep a safe distance.

But the insane ape is so large, and you are so small. It may be impossible to avoid. If it comes upon you in rage or silence, you must await your doom or strike as hard as you can, knowing it to be pointless. What hope has a single cell against the body impolitic?

Wren

I cannot but admire the poise of my evisceration,
hypnotic texture of her gaze, my many eyes seared
by each feather's inexorable grace.

As my chitin majestically unravels, a needle sharper
than time penetrates. She knows every inch of me,
and some in between.

I wonder if the man with the camera knows my fear,
my agony. That my whole life's purpose was to give
her strength to flap her wings a tiny bit faster a tiny
bit longer.

Cause

Best not to embrace a cause. You may find its
embrace gentle, even pleasing at first. Soon its grip
will strengthen, pull you in, crush you with unfath-
omable force until all you were or could be or meant
to be has been reduced to a homogenized puree,
which it then squeezes into a tube for distribution.
The cause does not do this from malice. It simply
does not realize the damage it causes, does not know
its own strength.

Or maybe it does.

Your Move

The world waits with bated breath.

What will you do? Such promise cannot go unfulfilled, such expectation cannot be unmet.

They won't.

The world knows you are biding your time, gathering your resources, mustering your resolve. It knows that when you do move it will be with strength, with greatness, with purpose. The world knows that, whether ennobled or debased, it never will be the same.

What great works will your genius weave? What new wisdom will it reveal? It's only a matter of time, for surely this is your destiny. That much is patent, that much is clear. All that remains is to work out the details. Only you can see to those.

What wonders and marvels will you show the world or take from it? Surely your deeds will resound through the ages. They will be sung as long as any remain to sing them, perhaps as rhapsody, perhaps as dirge.

How many of us are remembered in word, let alone song? You will be. It merely is a matter of what. And when.

The world waits with bated breath.

Your move, creep.

Thank you for reading
The Last Cloud

If you liked it,
please consider
writing a review on
Amazon or **Goodreads**

———————◆———————

Sign up for my newsletter
at **www.kmhalpern.com**
for information about
upcoming books and projects!
You will get exclusive
access to goodies such as
free chapters, stories,
and entry into a raffle to win
a set of books!

www.kmhalpern.com

ABOUT

K.M. Halpern was born in New York and, after spending far too much time there, finally returned to the Cambridge, MA, he knew and loved from graduate school. Unfortunately, it was nowhere to be found.

In its stead was a single large biotech complex, unfathomably wide and inconceivably long. Fortunately, zoning kept it from being unimaginably tall. The complex was owned by a shady hedge fund and hosted an indescribably large number of startups. Indescribable because the number has been patented by a fellow in Texas.

The startups competed for the next billion dollar patent, almost a whole month's rent. Specifically, they were trying to find a cure for an excess of optimism about biotech. Naturally, such a situation could not endure. The ground buckled, the markets balked, and the grand edifice collapsed with an astounding whimper. All that remains are a lot of people mumbling about unicorns and "it being just around the corner." Whether they refer to the rehab clinic or something else remains unknown.

Fortunately, K.M. survived the great collapse. The only way to tell him apart from the other crazy muttering people is that he mutters in pretentiously anachronistic language which one cannot help but imagine is affected.

K.M. Halpern holds a PhD in theoretical physics from the famous school "MIT pre-2000" — not to be confused with the similar sounding "MIT post-2000," a humanities satellite branch of Harvard. Nobody is sure where all the mathematicians and physicists went, but there is speculation they were absorbed by a black hole, which may be why people study black hole information theory.

K.M. may be found at www.kmhalpern.com, or out searching for the black hole where all the smart people went so he can yell at them for neglecting to invite him.

Other Works by K.M. Halpern

The Man Who Stands in Line

Killer flies, amorous dinosaurs, angry buildings, and one very large fish — all in a single volume. This quirky collection of flash fiction, vignettes, and poetry is variously absurd, dark, and comic. A monstrous blister, the secret to immortality, and a lost piece of brain are just a few other oddities one will encounter in this one-of-a-kind book.

"...the lasting impression of the writing within is without question. Don't let their brevity fool you; these works are tenacious, earnest, and overflowing with gloom."

— Kirkus Review

The Way Around

More absurd, horrifying, and downright inexplicable shorts from the mind of K.M. Halpern. Included are such soon-to-be classics as Buzz-Saw Bob, the sport of pendulum watching, yet another secret to ultimate success, the art of gasping, a neighbor who is definitely not Mr. Rogers, and Buddha's morning commute.

I legally can't promise that this book will transform you into the demiurge you were meant to be. All I can say is that no medical studies have proved otherwise and the FDA moves very slowly.

Available through Amazon, B&N, and bookstores everywhere.

Visit www.kmhalpern.com
Subscribe for updates, special offers, and bonus short stories!